To Bo

Every time you
about my book you
an encouragement to me.
Thanks!

Ruth O. Hatch

KNOW ME, HEAR ME, OBEY ME

By

Ruth G. Hatch

authorHOUSE™

1663 LIBERTY DRIVE, SUITE 200
BLOOMINGTON, INDIANA 47403
(800) 839-8640
WWW.AUTHORHOUSE.COM

First published by AuthorHouse 11/29/05

ISBN: 1-4208-9320-3 (sc)

Printed in the United States of America
Bloomington, Indiana

This book is printed on acid-free paper.

Do you know God? Can we know God? How does one get to know God? Who is God? What God do we want to know?

Spending time in God's presence is the way to get to know Him. The Bible says in Acts 3:19, "Repent therefore and be converted, that your sins may be blotted out, so that times of refreshing may come from the presence of the Lord, and that He may send Jesus Christ, who was preached to you before, whom heaven must receive until the restoration of all things, which God has spoken by the mouth of all His holy prophets since the world began.

How do we get to know anyone? By spending time with them. Talking with them. Asking questions and listening to them. John 17:3 says, "That they may know You, the only true God, and Jesus Christ whom You have sent". Ephesians 3:19 says, "To know the love of God". So, can we know God? Yes. John tells us we can know God. Which god? The only true God.

In Jeremiah 9:24 it says, "But let him who glories glory in this, that he understands and knows Me, That I am the Lord, exercising loving kindness, judgment, and righteousness in the earth. For in these I delight, says the Lord".

What makes us feel like we don't know God anyways? Sin separates us from God. When we repent of our sins, which is a turning away from them, God's presence comes to us. He removes the barrier from between us. I John 1: 9-2:2 says, "If we confess our sins, He is faithful and just to forgive us our sins and to cleanse us from all unrighteousness. If we say that we have not sinned, we make Him a liar, and His word is not in us. My little children, these things I write unto you, so that you may not sin. And if anyone sins, we have an advocate with the Father, Jesus Christ the righteous. And He Himself is the propitiation for our sins, and not for ours only, but also for the whole world".

Proverbs 8:34a says, "Blessed is the man who listens to me". God not only wants us to know Him, He wants us to hear Him when He speaks to us. O. K., You say, "How does God speak to us?" Well, there's a number of ways that He does. For one, we have the Bible, God's written word which we have available to us everyday. We also can listen to pastors or prophets which preach or give out God's word. Then, sometimes, He speaks to us through a friend or person who is close to us. At other times He speaks through a still small voice within. God never speaks to us something that is against His principles of the word. We need to try the spirit and make sure it is from God. That it's not something from a false spirit. I John 4:1 says, "Beloved, do not believe every spirit, but test the spirits, whether they are of God, because many false prophets have gone out into the world. By this you know the Spirit of God: Every spirit that confesses that Jesus Christ has come in the flesh is of God, and every spirit that does not confess that Jesus Christ has come in the flesh is not of God".

Lord, I'm Listening!

Go to your school and be a light. "Let your light so shine before men, that they will see your good works and glorify your Father in heaven" Matthew 5: 16. But God, I can't talk about you at school. I didn't say talk about me. I said let your light shine. What do you mean, let my light shine? I don't have a flash light attached to me or flames coming out of my head. I said, "*Let* your light shine. I didn't say *make* your light shine". But God...but God... Listen! If you have talked to me, admitted that you have done wrong, asked me to forgive you and cleanse you, then invited me into your life, you are a light. I am the light of the world. When I came into your life, you became a light. For a light to be very effective, it must be in a dark place. The darker the place the brighter the light shines. If you were to go into a very dark cave and strike a match, that light from the match immediately dispels the darkness. Immediately you can see. It's not dark. That's how you are. You are a light shinning in a dark place. When the light is shinning you can find your way.

Hear God! Bring the light where he tells you to bring it. Jesus said in John 8:7, "He who is of God hears God's words: Therefore you do not hear, because you are not of God". I don't know about you, but I don't want it to be said about me that I am not of God. I am bought with a price the precious blood of Jesus. I am sealed unto redemption. John 3:16 says, "For God so loved the world that He gave His only begotten Son that whosoever believeth in Him would have everlasting life".

II Corinthians 4:6 says, "For it is the God who commanded light to shine out of darkness who has shone in our hearts to give the light of the knowledge of the glory of God in the face of Jesus Christ."

Knowing God

When I was growing up, I attended a church that taught the Bible. I was taught about the God of Abraham, Isaac, Jacob. I learned about all the old Testament people and how God moved and worked in their lives. I learned about Jesus and His miracles in the New Testament. We talked about the death, resurrection and ascension into heaven of Jesus. I knew about God, Jesus, the Holy Spirit. I believed the Bible. I tried to follow it's guide lines.

When I was seventeen, my parents were going to go to Florida for the winter. Two years before we had gone to Florida. My dad bought a piece of land and cleared it. He had a small house built. My dad, mom and me moved into the house. We stayed in Florida until the end of the school year and went back to Maine. The next year we didn't go to Florida. I was glad. I had not been very happy during the time we were there. I missed all my friends both at church and school. I was quiet and pretty shy. I'm thankful for the friends I did make while I was there. I still have contact with two of them, Pat Wright and Elizabeth Duckworth. So, when I was seventeen and my parents decided to go to Florida again I really didn't want to go. I was dating Bill (my husband now). I didn't want to leave him. He didn't want me to leave either. We decided to get married. We talked to my parents and they agreed to sign for me to marry him, as I was underage.

We planned a very nice small church wedding. George P. Hendrickson performed the wedding ceremony. Augie and Shirley Lupino provided the special music. My brothers Tom and Warren were ushers. Roberta, my best friend, was my maid of honor and Bill's best friend, Oscar Maddox, was his best man. My niece Karen was our flower girl and my nephew Bob was our Ring bearer. We had a reception downstairs at the church with about 75 friends and relatives attending. We went for wedding pictures and we came back to the church and enjoyed the reception.

Later that evening we left for our honeymoon in Niagara Falls, New York and Canada. On our return trip we decided to stop in and see my sister Mary and her husband Lewis Schachne in New York City. The next day as it happens, my folks were on their way to Florida, their car developed some kind of problem as they were crossing the George Washington Bridge in New York. They called my sister also. They had to have the car towed to a garage. My folks ended up having Thanksgiving Dinner there in New York. Bill and I continued on our way home as my sister Cora and her husband Dave were expecting us for the evening meal on Thanksgiving. I guess my sister Mary had plenty of excitement on that Thanksgiving Day.

Three months later, I went to the doctor and received the news that we were expecting our first child, Sue. We were living in an apartment on Main St. in Springvale, Maine owned by Fred Gowen and his wife. Right near

Gowen's Park. Shortly after, Bill's father became ill. We moved in with him to help care for him until he died a year later.

In my late teens, early twenties, I started to move into another life style. I stopped attending church and started to go my own way. In just a few months my marriage was falling apart. I was involved in an adulterous relationship and wanted to walk out on my husband and three small children.

God intervened. An elderly couple from the church, John and Ethel King came to visit us. They encouraged us to get right with God and come back to church. I started attending church again where I asked for God's forgiveness. I also asked Him to come into my life and take control. I asked Him to do in me what I could not do in my self. That day, He changed me forever. "Therefore, if anyone is in Christ, he is a new creation: old things have passed away: behold, all things have become new" II Corinthians 5:18, 19 says it so well.

How can we know God? Through Jesus Christ His Son. Some say there are many ways to God. Well, they must be talking about another god. There is only one way to the true and living God. The God who created the universe. The one who created man in His likeness. The God of Abraham, Isaac, and Jacob. The God that brought the fire down when Elijah prayed over the altar with the barrels of water poured over it. The God who shut the mouths of the lions to save Daniel. The God who opened the Red Sea to save the Israelites. The God who raised Lazarus from the dead. The God who caused a great fish to swallow Jonah and spit him up on land again. (Whoops, You mean you believe in that) Yep! The same God that cleansed the ten lepers. The same one that caused the blind man to see. "Neither is there salvation in any other: for there is none other name under heaven given amongst men, whereby we must be saved" Acts 4:12.

It is Jesus! Oh! It is Jesus! It is Jesus in my soul. For I have touched the hem of His garment and His blood has made me whole. This is the words of a song I sang many times as a young person. The words remain with me as I age and mean more to me than ever.

Have you reached out and touched Him, like the woman in the Bible did? She had a physical need for twelve years and when Jesus was passing by she reached the hem of His clothing. She was made whole. Another time in the Bible, Jesus told a man to go in peace your sins are forgiven you. Some religious leaders were upset. They said, How can He forgive sin? That is blasphemy. They didn't understand that He was the Son of God and He could forgive sin as well as heal. As the fullness of God was upon Him, He had the power and authority not only to heal, but to forgive their sins.

I talk to my best friend, Jesus. When I'm sad I say, "Here I am. It's me again". He always listens. When I'm afraid, He comforts. When I walk a loved one to the door of death, He is there with His arms around me. When I have a problem I can't seem to solve, He either helps bring a solution or helps me through the frustration of having no answer. I'm so glad I *KNOW* Him.

Knowing God through His Son Jesus is a growing process. Yes, there is an initial commitment to know Christ. The new birth experience. It is a choice, but it is more than that. God's spirit comes into us giving us new life. There is a change. "If anyone is in Christ, he is a new creation; old things are passed away; behold, all things have become new" II Corinthians 5:17. He forgives us of our sin and cleanses us. We can now have fellowship with Him. I John 1:7-10 says, "But if we walk in the light, as He is in the light, we have fellowship one with another, and the blood of Jesus Christ His Son cleanses us from all sin. If we say we have not sinned, we make Him a liar, and His word is not in us. Romans 3:6 says, "For the wages of sin is death, but the gift of God is eternal life in Christ Jesus our Lord.

When I first knew God, I used to read a little devotional book that was handed out at my church I attended. It was called *God's Word For Today*. It had a scripture portion and a little story to emphasize the point of the scripture verse. I couldn't get over how many times the scripture and story were relevant to what was going on in my life. I believe it was a way that God was speaking to me. He was leading me or confirming his will in my life.

Hear Me

We can know God but, we will never learn all there is to know about God. It is a life time experience of knowing, learning and growing. If we stop learning and growing, we're dead! I would hope for my entire life I will continue to learn and grow mentally, emotionally and spiritually.

When I was in my early teens I remember thinking about going on to school to teach. I ended up choosing another route, at least for the time being. I married and raised three children. As my oldest daughter was graduating from high school and made plans to go to college, I signed up for some classes at a local community college in the small New England town where I lived in Sanford,

Maine. I had quit high school in my senior year but, later I went back and got my GED. The college let me take classes as long as I maintained at least a C average. I got mostly A's so I could continue. When I started, I thought I would get an A.A. Degree in Geriatrics. I enjoyed working with older people and helping them deal with the various circumstances that arise in their lives. I did a practicum at two nursing homes in my home town working with the social workers and the activity directors in both places.

About this time my mother got to the point where she needed to have someone help her out some. We had invited her to come stay with us. She was still ambulatory and able to care for herself. She could bath and dress herself. She could come to the table and eat. She was able to use the bathroom on her own. It was mainly a matter of having someone around and she didn't have to cook meals or try to do washing which she had a hard time to do.

One day my mother wasn't feeling well. She stayed in bed. I brought her meals to her. The next day she wasn't feeling well again. I called her doctor. He was planning to come and check on her before noon. I called my brother Ray. He came to the house and talked to her. We went in the kitchen and talked for a while. Then, we went back in to mom. Ray noticed that she didn't seem to be breathing. I checked for a pulse and couldn't find one. We called the ambulance. They came and tried to revive her. They took her to the hospital but, they were not able to revive her. She was gone.

I was thankful that God allowed me this time with my mom. We had long talks about things from years pass. I got to know her in a greater way than I had ever known her before. She would ask about each of my brothers and sisters. There was still four of my six brothers living. One had passed away when I was only months old from cancer. Alfred, he was in the Air Force. My brother Earl had passed away a few years before. He had a faulty heart valve. The doctors had successfully replaced it with a pig's valve, but he died from other complications. Both of my sisters Cora and Mary were still living. My mother and dad had 10 children. One was still born. There were nine of us, eleven with mom and dad. Quite a family. It was great when we all got together for Thanksgiving or Mom's or Dad's birthday and other special occasions. Mom and Dad would pray for us all regularly. I believe that had a lot to do with the fact that we all became good, upright, productive people in our various communities. Dad had died ten years earlier than mom. Mom had lived alone until she came to stay with us that last year. Both Mom and Dad were strong willed people and determined. They both loved God and relied on Him for strength and guidance. I remember hearing Dad sing the words of a beloved hymn, "And He walks with me and He talks with me and He tells me I am His own". I believe the name of it is, *In The Garden.*

Mom had made her peace with God and was ready to go to be with Him and Dad. A couple years later, when my brother Ray died of cancer, I had a dream of Mom and Dad. I was sitting in a room and they came to the window and looked in and said, "Hello, how are you?" At first I was shocked. Then, I was glad to see them. Then, I woke up. It was as if God let them come say hello and comfort me during this time of grief. It was very comforting.

About two weeks before Mom had passed away, my husband Bill and I were talking. We had felt God leading us to go to Alaska and visit a church that our church in Maine was helping support. We wanted to go but, we didn't have the finances for the trip. We had prayed and said, "Lord", if you want us to go you'll provide the finances for the trip". Two weeks later Mom died. One night right after mom had passed away we were awake. I was crying and grieving. I knew she was with the Lord. But, it still hurt and I missed her. We had been to the reading of the will that day. Bill reminded me that with the money my mom had left us, we could make the trip to the church in Alaska.

A few months later after contacting the church and pastor in Alaska, we made the trip to Palmer, Alaska. We flew into Anchorage. We spent our first night there in Anchorage with some friends that had moved to Anchorage from Maine. We woke up in the morning to a loud roaring sound. At first, I thought a train or a jet was near by. As we were still lying in bed, I heard our friend call to her husband that we were having an earthquake. She said, "Should I get everyone out of the house? The water is splashing out of the fish tank." He was up stairs talking a shower. I remember thinking, *"God, You didn't bring us up here to kill us in an earthquake"*. Suddenly, I felt very peaceful. The earthquake stopped. If I remember right, it was a 7.2; However, it didn't cause a lot of damage. It knocked things off shelves in stores. It didn't hurt the roads, because later in the day we went ahead and drove up to Palmer.

At the church in Palmer we sang and gave our testimony. While we were singing, several people came to the altar to pray. We talked some people afterwards. One man in particular stood out to me. He said he and his wife had separated but, he felt God spoke to him that day and told him to go back and make things right with her. I pray that he did. I believe that God did other things there that we never knew about. The important thing is that we listened to God and did what we believed He told us to do.

I believe God spoke to us by His Spirit to go there and tell the people that God loved them. I argued with God. I said, "But God, they have a pastor. There's other people much closer to them then we are that could go". But He said, "I would like you to go". Sometimes it seems to take something out of the ordinary, like someone traveling several thousand miles to tell them. I wished I didn't argue with God and could get to the point where *He Speaks, I Listen and I Do.*

God did the ultimate thing for us to show His love by sending His Son Jesus but, sometimes we need someone to tell us, or show us. God help us to be listening to you.

Obey Me

When I was in my fourties, I was at a fellowship supper one night at our church. I was sitting across from my friend Nancy Lambert. A family in our church that had taken in many foster children, were such a blessing in our church, were moving away. The father's job situation was taking the family out of state to live and work.

Our pastor, Pastor Jim McAtee told how the mom would go down to an area where the church was thinking of purchasing land to build a new church and she would pray. He made a challenge. Who would stand in the gap and pray? My friend Nancy looked at me and said, "We could". She asked if I wanted to join her in praying. I said I would.

Nancy and I started calling each other to go down to the land that the church had bought by now. We would pray for the finances. We would pray for the right workers. We would pray for every detail we could think of for the church. We prayed that every part of the church building would be ordained by God. We prayed for the pastor, the board of deacons, the Sunday School Workers, the music department, singers, musicians, anything that had to do with the church. We would pray for various needs of people that we were aware of in the church or out of the church. Nancy's dad had been a pastor, so she thought of things that I would never have thought of to pray for. That God would intervene in the lives of individuals

As the church started to be built, it was amazing how, if there were finances needed, we would pray and see finances come in as needed. If workmen were needed, we would see workmen come. When an architect was needed, one showed up.

Winter came and the first part of the building was capped off. Nancy and I would go down to the property. Sometimes the snowplows had gone by and plowed up a huge snow bank, but we could climb over the bank. We would go down the steps into the basement with the cap over us and pray. We would pray until we were too cold to stay there any more. We would have to leave. A couple of times the snow was too deep to trudge through, so we sat in the vehicle by the road side and prayed. This went on for months. We would go and pray, pray, pray. Spring came and the church went forward. The church was built.

We had one room where we met once a week for prayer. We had asked the pastor if we could start a Tuesday morning prayer group. He came back and gave us the O.K.. We decided on the next Tuesday to start. By now, there were three or four of us coming together.

That first Tuesday, for some reason the others couldn't make it and I was there by myself. I felt really discouraged. I had felt that God wanted us to do this and it seemed it wasn't going to happen. I said, "O. K

. ,God, if you want this to keep going, at least let one other person come pray with me". In about ten minutes an elderly lady, Mary Johnson came and we prayed. After that, we had from six to as many as thirty ladies who gathered to pray. We also encouraged each one to pray during the week.

We started keeping a prayer journal on the prayers for various people and needs. Then we would record when the prayer was answered. I remembered some prayers got answered before the next week. Some took two or three years. Some longer. I have since moved away from that area, but I still keep in contact with friends there. The Tuesday morning prayer group is still meeting, almost twenty years later.

One thing I learned, it's amazing how urgent a thing can be when someone brings a need or concern to you for prayer, but sometimes after God wonderfully meets the need it can become a small thing. God help us to be thankful and grateful to You for every answered prayer. I believe prayer is mostly us lining up with what God wants, and us getting a clearer view of His will.

"That I might know Him and the power of His resurrection" Phil. 4:10. The power of His resurrection. When you think of it. Can you imagine the power it takes to bring life to something. If you were with a loved one and they pass on. Can you imagine then if they came back to life? Impossible! Lazarus did. Jesus raised him from the dead. With God all things are possible. So maybe you could accept the possibility of that person raising from the dead. This has been known to happen. I talked with a lady at our church. Her husband had been mowing the lawn and collapsed. She called 911, but she kept praying. They came and worked on him. They said he was dead and she said, keep doing what you're doing and she kept praying. They loaded him in the ambulance and took him to the hospital. He started breathing again. He is fine. He was home the next day and an ambulance driver saw him in the yard. He said, "Aren't you the man we pronounced dead yesterday?" He said, "Yes Sir". It's been a year or more since that happened. He sits near us in church every Sunday.

What about a block of wood? Could that raise up and be living once again? You say, O.K. You're getting far out now. A block of wood was once living. Could it be raised to life again. All right. "No". A block of wood could not be raised to life. All right. Could someone take a handful of dirt mold it, breath into it and it becomes a living breathing soul? Yes! Someone did. God! This is a glimpse of resurrection power. If that person died and was brought back to life, which is more difficult? To fix a car, or to make a car from scratch and get it running? God has a great desire for us to know Him and the power of His resurrection

To Know God! What does it mean, to know God?

Let's examine what it means to know someone. Sometimes we are introduced to someone. We see them at a later time and say " Yeah, I know them". Maybe we met them at such and such place on a certain date. Well. What do they do for work? Well, I don't know. Do they have children? I don't know. You say you met them. You were introduced to them. Maybe even were told a few things about them, but you don't *know* them.

To know someone takes some time. Spend some time with them. Talk to them. Talk with others about them. Listen to other peoples stories about them. In time, you can say you *know* them.

This word *know,* has an even deeper meaning than that. In the Bible, the word *know meant* to have an intimate knowledge of someone, or to have sex with them. In other words, to have a very intimate relationship with that person. God wants a very intimate relationship, not to have sex, but to spend time alone with us. He wants us to listen to Him. He wants us to get to know how He thinks and feels. What He wants and likes. He wants us to *know Him, to hear Him and to obey Him.*

Know Me   Hear Me
Obey Me

We the church are the bride of Christ. This is the intimate relationship He wants with us. I saw and heard a beautiful illustration of this a few years ago here in Deland, Florida, by my pastor's wife Renee Modica. She spoke about how we are Christ's bride. She had a beautiful, white wedding dress, but she dunked it in a pail of muddy dirty water. She told about how we get stained with sinful practices, lying, cheating, adulterous, etc. She tore the dress and she said we become tattered and torn. She held up the gown all dirty and torn and she said, "That's how we have become". She told how Jesus comes to us, accepts us back, cleanses us from sin and makes us beautiful and clean. At the end, a bride in a beautiful pure white gown came down the middle isle of the church. At the front of the church stood a man portraying Jesus. When she got to Him, He took her by the hand and they waked up into an area that looked like clouds, to be with Him. He wants that close relationship with us. Now! Come to Him.

About sixteen years ago my husband and I were living in another state. Our children were all grown and two were married. I was very active in church working with a prayer group and having a fellowship group for the seniors, but I allowed a sin to come into my life that shouldn't have been there. I was feeling very guilty. My husband had been working for a company for 24 years. One day he came home and said he'd like to retire and move to Florida. This was quite a shock. He was not a person given to sudden changes. He was pretty much a home body and liked to keep things the way they always have been. We started to talk about moving. We prayed about it and we decided to start taking steps to fulfill this decision. My heart was torn. I was excited about the new adventure, but sad to leave family and friends.

We had been to Florida earlier in the year to visit our daughter Sue and her husband Ted. We had looked for land to build on, when we retired. We were not planning to move right away. We had found land and we decided to purchase it; however, once we got home we decided to put our house up for sale and see what would happen. The first people that looked at it bought it. They didn't want to move in right away. They were going to get married in the fall and would move in then. That was perfect. We rented the house from them for a couple of months till we were ready to move. In the mean time I flew to Florida found a modular home that I bought and went back to Maine. Everything seemed to be working out perfectly.

On the third week of August we loaded all our belongings into a rented truck and headed for Florida. Our son David came with us to help drive the truck, as we had it and our car. It would be fourteen hundred miles. It took us three days of driving all day each day to get to Paisley, Florida. We were all exhausted.

I had talked to the sales person that I purchased the modular home from just days before we started out. He had assured me that the home would be on the land and we could just back our truck up and unload everything. Well ! We got there and no house….. Here we were fourteen hundred miles away from family and friends. We were not happy campers. We had no place to put our stuff. We had everything we owned in a rented truck, that we were going to have to turn in in a couple of days. We had got a hold of the man we bought our modular home from. They had run into some snags. They were not able to have the house there. Obviously! We had to go find a storage place that you could rent and unload everything into it. The temperatures were running about ninety-five degrees. We were not used to this kind of heat. Eighty was hot to us.

Now we had to figure out where we were going to stay till they would get our house set up. They said it would be a matter of days. It ended up taking five weeks before we could move in to our house. The closest motel was twelve miles away in another town. We were able to get an efficiency room and pay by the week or month. This was a very upsetting time in our lives.

The man that we bought the modular home from was responsible for our home not being set up as promised. So, he paid for the five weeks we were in the motel until our house was brought in and set up. This was a very low point in our lives. We were angry at our selves, at the man for not doing what he said. I think at this point we were mad at the world. I was feeling very guilty for the sin in my life. We had moved away from all our friends and relatives. We didn't seem to have anyone to encourage us at this point and our relationship with God was not what it should have been. I didn't even feel like I could ask Him to help. (As I look back now as I write this, I realize there were people who encouraged us. I didn't always see it at the time.)

We had to do a lot of running around to get things straight for the house. This wasn't always easy. Our land was in a small town called Paisley. It was twenty miles to the closest town that had any of the stores and other things we were used to having near us. The county seat was about twenty five miles, which we had to travel there often to complete different permits that were needed.

A man named Claud Bowers and his wife Freeda had started a Christian T.V. station up in Leesburg, Florida, which is now in Orlando. I would turn in and watch this station. They were struggling with the new beginning. I could definitely identify with them. We were struggling with a new beginning, also.

We started to attend a small Baptist Church in Paisley, Florida. Pastor Butler and his wife Barbara were very nice to us. They even let us come to their house and take showers, when we had a problem with our well, right after we moved in. The sand caved in and we had to have a new well drilled about 2 weeks after we finally moved into our house. The day after we got our well hooked up a truck delivering our back steps for the house, backed up and got stuck in the sand. The truck driver kept spinning his wheels and dug down to our water pipe that came from the well to our house and broke it. Water was shooting everywhere. We had to shut the water off. A neighbor came down with his tractor and pulled the truck out of the sand. Then we had to go get some more piping and pout a piece of new pipe in to fix it.

We got our water back; however, when I came home and our water had just got hooked up, I was excited. I set my purse on the back of the car and went over to see what was happening. I came back and went into the house. Bill had to run to the store later. When we were getting ready to go to church that night, I went to get my purse. No purse. I couldn't find it. We finally went to church anyways. We looked along the road going to church. We figured it must have fallen off the car. We told the people at church what had happened. After church many people helped us look for my purse, but we could not find it. We figured someone found it and kept the money.

The next day we got a call from the post office in Paisley. Someone had turned my purse in there. We didn't have a street address, just a post office box number. So the post office called us. Thank God! We got everything back. I had about one hundred dollars, several important papers, as I had just been to get my Florida drivers license.

Even after we moved from the motel to our house we were only able to get a couple channels on our T.V.. One of which was Channel 55. I thank God for the encouragement we received through that channel and the programming they bring to our area.

After we got settled in our home, we needed to find work. I saw an add in the paper for orange packers at a local plant. I decided to go put in an application. I had worked in an apple packing plant years before. It was something I had had some experience in doing. After I filled out the application, the person checking it noticed I had some college. She asked if I would be interested in a job in the lab. She said they would train me it I was interested. I said yes. I started the next day. The training was on the day shift. That wasn't bad. I found out I took the place of a person that got done because her husband got killed out in the blending room in the plant. Apparently he was in a blender cleaning it and someone accidentally turned it on. It gave me the chills every time I would think about it.

Working in the lab was interesting. I was amazed at all the tests done on juice to make sure it was safe and top quality; however, I didn't like having to go out into the plant to get the samples of juice and pulp. I had to climb around by some grinders that seemed dangerous. They didn't always have the safety covers closed. You could slip and get hurt badly. I also had to go up on some high cat walks. I didn't care for that either.

Finally, I was off training and started working on my own. I was put on night shift. I had a hard time to work nights and stay awake. I had trouble sleeping in the day time.

Bill, my husband hadn't found work, so he came to the juice plant also. He was hired to work up in the bins. Trucks would come in and dump the oranges and he would make sure they kept rolling down the ramp. He had to be careful. It was easy to slip and fall. One man did fall and break his leg. This was a difficult time. Bill was working hard. When the oranges were coming in fast, he worked for 21 days without a day off. They said they could do that since it was agriculture. I thought it was against the law. We were thankful for work and we were able to pay our bills. We both were working hard. We had long hours each week at the juice plant.

During the coming months and years we got more involved in the small church we were attending Sometimes we faced skepticisms and criticisms. We had both grown up in and attended an Assemblies of God Church. There were a few people who would chide us about this as we were attending a Baptist Church now. There were only two churches in Paisley. A Baptist Church and a Methodist Church. We had decided to try the Methodist Church. We decided to go one Sunday night. We pulled into the parking lot and waited for other people to come before going in. Finally someone came in the parking lot and came over to us and said, "Oh, this is the fifth Sunday night. We go over to the Baptist Church for a combined singspiration". They said to come on over. So we went. We ended up attending that church for approximately twelve years. We felt we would like to support our local church and not drive twenty miles to find another. So we did. We became very involved in the church there in Paisley.

Pastor Butler and his wife Barbara were very supportive. One day the pastor spoke about having nothing between us and God. Not even one thing. The Holy Spirit dealt with me about the sin I had had in my life. He showed me I needed to confess it to my husband. I had all ready confessed it to God and knew He had forgiven me, but the Holy Spirit showed me I needed to talk to Bill about it and make sure things were right between us as husband and wife. I talked to him. I confessed to him. God did a beautiful healing in our marriage. He gave us a renewed love for each other after almost 30 years of marriage. If you want a good marriage you have to keep working at it. Never stop working at it.

It's been over 40 years now and it gets sweeter every day with God's help. During the years we lived in this small town in Florida, we grew spiritually. We didn't have our family and friends around. We had to make new friends. This seemed to be a slow process. We lived there a few years before I finally had a friend that I felt close to and could talk openly with.

My new friend was our Bible Study teacher at church. Her and I would get together and take long walks. We were trying to watch our weight. During these walks we would have some good talks and we would encourage each other. One day she said she wasn't going to be able to walk that afternoon because her mom was going to be away. She was going over to feed her mom's dog. That day when I came home, Bill and I sat down to eat dinner. The phone rang. It was another person from church calling to say my friend Mary had been killed early that morning. She had been at work and got on a fork lift. She had driven one for eleven years, but she had recently been promoted to foreman and didn't usually drive it any more. Apparently, someone had not come in that night. She jumped on to one and was going up a ramp. The fork lift went off the edge of the ramp and flipped over on top of her. It crushed her head and she died instantly. I was shocked and stunned. It wouldn't sink in at first. The person hung up. Bill put his arms around me and consoled me. Mary was a wonderful, bubbly person. Her face would shine with God's presence. I had to remind myself that she was with the Lord. Would she want me to wish that away? I missed her very much, but I realized that she was where I will be one day. In the arms of Jesus.

Mary's husband had a very difficult time. He would go sit at the cemetery for hours. At one point, he wanted to kill himself, but he finally made it through. We've moved away from that town now and we have lost contact with him, but I know that God is sufficient. I'm glad that Mary knew Jesus. I know she did because we talked about it and she told me that she accepted Christ as her personal Savior. She asked Him to forgive her sins and come in to her life.

How about you? Do you know Christ and His forgiveness? You can, even now. Just talk to Him. Ask Him to forgive you and cleanse you. Ask Him to change you and make you a new person. The Bible says in II Corinthians 5:17, Therefore, if any man be in Christ he is a new creature, old things are passed away; behold, all things are become new". You can be born again.

The Bible says you must be born again. In the book of St. John, chapter 3, Jesus said, "Except a man be born again, he can not see the kingdom of God". What must I do? "Believe on the Lord Jesus Christ and thou shalt be saved and thy house" Acts 16:31. Saved from the punishment of sin.

Our daughter Charity called a few days ago. It's always good to hear from our children. She lives over 1400 miles away in Saco, Maine. She told me about a lady she met at the hospital where she is an registered nurse. She said this lady began telling her about going to a Bible study at a woman's house. She named the street and house where she went. She said the lady talked to her and prayed with her. She said the lady said. "She saved my life". Apparently, this person was thinking of taking her life, but God led her to this Bible study on, "Lord, Change Me" by Evelyn Christianson. I was doing this Bible study and became very discouraged. Not many people came and I felt like it had been a failure. God choose to let me hear about this after about 20 years. I'm so glad I listened to the Lord and did the study. It goes to show we just never know what God is doing.

Even when things don't seem to be going the way we think they should.

This week I got a call from a former pastor of ours. He said their church pianist's son had been killed in a car crash and would I come play the piano for the memorial service. I said I'd be glad to go. The son had known the Lord and the service was more of a celebration of his graduation to be with the Lord. It was a very sweet time to renew old acquaintances and meet with friends we hadn't seen for a while. The family said it was really a blessing to know he was with the Lord. He had had a lot of physical problems. He was going to have several surgeries, but now they know he won't have any more pain or sickness. They also know they will one day see him again on that great reunion day. Praise God!

Many times the Holy Spirit will lead us or nudge us to do something. We may not know why, but it's important to hear and obey. Sometimes He may choose to tell us why. Sometimes we may never know why. He will never tell us to do anything that goes against His word, the Bible.

During the time we lived in Paisley I started working in a private facility for the mentally and physically handicapped people, the Duval Home, as an instructor. When I was in Maine, the last two years, I worked as a teacher's assistant in the public schools. I worked in a Special Education Class for Educable Mentally Handicapped Students. Between my college work and the experience I had, it qualified me for this position. I worked there for a year and a half. I became very tired and depressed. I got done for several months. Then, one day I got up and felt impressed to go back to work there. The Director of Education Training there said if I had come at any other time she wouldn't have been able to hire me. They had had a freeze on hiring. Apparently they put it back the day after they hired me. I stayed there another almost five years. This was a very influential time in my life. I learned some very important lessons in life working with children and adults that needed a lot of love, care and understanding. It made me realize the extent of God's love. He will go to great lengths to show us His love.

I enrolled back in college. I was also working full time. Eventually, I got a position as a teacher's assistant in the public school system. I worked in the ESE Department. (Exceptional Student Education Department) This was very helpful as I needed to observe many different classes. The experience working in the class room was very beneficial. I got to work with three different teachers who all had different styles of teaching. I learned much from each one of them, as well as from the students I worked with.

During the time I was attending school full time nights and Saturdays, working full time and being quite active in the little church we attended serving as Sunday School Director and later as Church Pianist for five years. I know God gave me grace and strength to do this.

Eventually I graduated with a Bachelors of Science Degree. I got certified in Varying Exceptionalities and I got a position teaching a self-contained Varying Exceptionalities Class at Deland Middle School in Deland, Florida. I believe God opened doors and led me to this position. He gives me strength and patience each and every day. I pray for my students and co-workers. I see God work every day.

At a very busy time at school, I got a call from my son, Dave, that live 1400 miles a way. He has a mentally handicapped daughter. She went to school and complained that her bottom was hurting. The teacher sent her to the school nurse. They did not let her go home that day. Children's Services put her in a temporary home. My son got a lawyer. They had brought charges against his wife. I flew up for the conferences. This is what they called them. They were not court dates. At one point Children's Services were going to take the other children, but they decided they were in no danger. There would be another conference to make a final decision. After their daughter had been out of the home for several weeks, she had to be hospitalized. She had a behavior of picking at her skin and making it bleed. Sometimes it gets pretty severe. This behavior started after a change in her medicines. She did have a behavior of pulling strings on her clothes, to the point of making her clothes fall apart. They had stopped all visitation to the hospital because of her condition. During the hospital stay the doctors took her off all medication. Instead of putting her in the temporary foster home, Children's Services put her in a children's home. They gave her father visiting privileges and then added visiting rights for her brothers and sisters. Through a lot of prayer from grandma's and grandpa's, friends and relatives, classes that mom and dad went through. She is now back home with her family.

The title of this book came to me one night during church service at our church. I was in the choir singing. The presence of the Lord was really sweet and heavy. Many people were crying and praying. Some were sitting, some standing. I sat down because I felt God's presence so strong. I couldn't stand. As I had my head down I began to think these words over and over. "Know Me, Hear Me, Obey Me". I kept thinking them over and over. Finally I said, "Lord, what are you trying to tell me?" I believe He said, "This is the title of the book I want you to write. I need to explain this a little bit. One morning previously, I had awaken, I was laying in bed. I looked up and saw myself, just like a cartoon picture. I was sitting at a table writing. I remember thinking, I'm seeing this and I know I'm not dreaming. I kept asking God in prayer what this meant. I didn't receive an answer for several months. Finally during this church service when these words were going over and over in my mind, I asked God what He was telling me. He said, This is the title of the book you will write. You have to understand. I am a nobody. I'm not famous. I'm the type of person people seem to look right past to say Hell to someone else.

God began to speak to my heart. He reminded me that He loved each and every one of us so much that He bleed and died for each one of us. He loved me. He loves you. He paid a huge price. When I saw the movie, "The Passion of Christ", by Mel Gibson recently, it reminded me a fresh and anew that He loves us so much. John 3:16 says, "For God so loved the world that He gave His only begotten Son, that everlasting life. God came not into the world to condemn the world, but that the world through Him might be saved. I

I believe no matter what point we're at in life, we can give ourselves over to God. We can ask for forgiveness from Him through His Son and we can become right with God. If we don't ask for His forgiveness, there is a great chasm between us and God. When we ask Him to forgive us of our sin, no matter what it may be, He will forgive us. This is a bridge over the chasm to God. Forgiveness through God's Son Jesus Christ is the bridge to God. A way to God when there was no way. We become adopted in to the family of God. We may have felt like a nobody, but now we are a child of God. We're one of His children. He cares about us intimately. The Bible says, "If you then, being evil, know how to give good gifts to your children, how much more will your Father who is in heaven give good things to those who ask Him!" Matthew 7:11.

If you have never prayed and asked for forgiveness. Do it today. He will forgive you and cleanse you from all your sin. You can have a fresh start. He gives us a new start in life. If someone asks, what about those things in the past, you can say, they are under the blood of Jesus. He has forgiven me. I am a different person. From this day forward, I will live for and serve Jesus. I will live by the principles of the Bible. I will find a good church and worship and gather regularly with other believers. The Bible calls this fellowship. You will be encouraged and you can encourage others.

There are many other things I could write about and perhaps will. I trust this will encourage you and it may be a means of you coming to know Jesus Christ as your personal Lord and Savior. If you know Him, I pray you will be encouraged. If you don't know Him, I pray you will stop right now and pray. Talk to Jesus. Ask for forgiveness. Commit your life to Him. Walk with Him daily. Read a Bible. God Bless You! *Know Him, Hear Him, Obey Him.* For He is saying, " Know Me, Hear Me, Obey Me!"

Printed in the United States
41109LVS00001B/205-354